THIS WALKER BOOK BELONGS TO:

_____

_____

_____

_____

Jack and the Beanstalk

Jack be Nimble

Jack be nimble,
Jack be quick,
Jack jump over
The candlestick.

Jack and Jill

Jack and Jill went up the hill
To fetch a pail of water;
Jack fell down and broke his crown,
And Jill came tumbling after.

The House that Jack Built

This is the farmer sowing his corn
that kept the cock that crowed in the morn
that waked the priest all shaven and shorn
that married the man all tattered and torn
that kissed the maiden all forlorn
that milked the cow with the crumpled horn
that tossed the dog that worried the cat
that killed the rat that ate the malt
that lay in the house that Jack built.

Little Jack Horner

Little Jack Horner
Sat in the corner,
Eating a Christmas pie;
He put in his thumb,
And pulled out a plum,
And said, What a good boy am I!

First published 1993 by Walker Books Ltd
87 Vauxhall Walk, London SE11 5HJ

This revised edition published 2001

2 4 6 8 10 9 7 5 3

© 1993, 2001 Catherine and Laurence Anholt

This book has been typeset in Plantin

Printed in Hong Kong

British Library Cataloguing in Publication Data:
a catalogue record for this book
is available from the British Library

ISBN 0-7445-8289-X

Come Back, JACK!

Catherine and Laurence Anholt

WALKER BOOKS

AND SUBSIDIARIES

LONDON • BOSTON • SYDNEY

There was once a girl who didn't like books.
Her mum liked books. Her dad liked books.
Her brother, Jack, *loved* books and he
couldn't even read.

"Books are boring," said the girl.
"I'm going outside to find a *real* adventure."

"Keep an eye on Jack!" called her mum.
But the girl didn't keep an eye on Jack.

She searched around for something
interesting. When she wasn't looking
Jack took off his shoes and socks and …

crawled right inside his book!
"Oh no!" said the girl. "COME BACK, JACK!"

But it was too late, Jack had already gone.
So the girl took off her shoes and socks
and crawled right in after him.

Inside the book was a steep green hill.
At the bottom someone was crying.

"Oh dear!" said the girl. "Now Jack has hurt himself."

But it wasn't Jack crying at the bottom of the hill. It was Jill.

"Jack fell down – and now he's run away," Jill said.

"Oh no!" said the girl, and she shouted, **"COME BACK, JACK!"**

The girl ran further into the book. After a few pages, she came to a funny house with a strange crowd outside.

"This is the house that Jack built," said a cow with a crumpled horn.

"Don't be silly," said the girl. Jack isn't old enough to build houses, he can't even read yet."

"Oh, he's a clever lad," said the cow. "Very nimble and quick, too. You just watch him jumping over that candlestick!"

"Oh no!" shouted the girl. And she shouted louder than ever ...

"COME BACK, JACK!"

The girl jumped so high she found herself way up in the clouds. She couldn't see Jack. What she could see was a huge castle with its enormous door wide open.

She crept inside ... and there was Jack, sitting in a corner, eating a Christmas pie. She was just about to tell him to take out his thumb and eat politely, when the whole castle began to shake.

A great voice roared,

"FEE FI FO FUM,

I'D REALLY LIKE TO EAT SOMEONE!"

Quick as a flash, the girl grabbed Jack's hand and ran out of the castle. But the giant had seen them. He shouted,

"FUM FO FEE FI, I WANT THOSE CHILDREN IN A PIE!"

And the other thing he yelled, in a great big giant voice was,

"COME BACK, JACK!"

Just in time, they found a beanstalk growing
up through the clouds. They started to climb
down, but the giant was getting closer.
He was about to grab them when ...

they reached the end of the book and tumbled out into their very own garden.

The giant's huge hairy hand reached out after them, but Jack banged the book shut.

From inside the book came a teeny, tiny roar,

"FEE FI FO FUM, NOW I'VE GONE AND HURT MY THUMB."

"Well," said the girl, "perhaps books aren't so boring after all!"

Then she and Jack lay on the grass, and they laughed and laughed and laughed.

And from inside the book came a faraway roar, "COME BACK, JACK!"

Jack and the Beanstalk

Jack be Nimble

Jack be nimble,
Jack be quick,
Jack jump over
The candlestick.

Jack and Jill

Jack and Jill went up the hill
To fetch a pail of water;
Jack fell down and broke his crown,
And Jill came tumbling after.

The House that Jack Built

This is the farmer sowing his corn
that kept the cock that crowed in the morn
that waked the priest all shaven and shorn
that married the man all tattered and torn
that kissed the maiden all forlorn
that milked the cow with the crumpled horn
that tossed the dog that worried the cat
that killed the rat that ate the malt
that lay in the house that Jack built.

Little Jack Horner

Little Jack Horner
Sat in the corner,
Eating a Christmas pie;
He put in his thumb,
And pulled out a plum,
And said, What a good boy am I!

CATHERINE and LAURENCE ANHOLT say of
Come Back, Jack!, "It is a NOISY story – we have
read it aloud to big groups of children, and when
two hundred kids yell, 'COME BACK, JACK!' at
the top of their voices, everyone knows about it for
miles around! The idea came from the expression
'lost in a book'. The cover of a book is a door into
a magical world – you knock on the front, take off
your shoes and socks (so the pages don't get dirty!),
then you step right inside… "

Catherine and Laurence Anholt are one of the UK's
leading author/illustrator teams, with over sixty
books to their credit. You can find out more about
the couple and their books by visiting their Website
(http:www.anholt.co.uk). They live and work in a
rambling farmhouse (haunted of course!)
in Lyme Regis, Dorset.

Other books by Catherine and Laurence Anholt

Twins, Two by Two 0-7445-6068-3 (p/b) £4.99
What I Like 0-7445-6070-5 (p/b) £4.99
What Makes Me Happy? 0-7445-6069-1 (p/b) £4.99
Here Come the Babies 0-7445-6066-7 (p/b) £4.99
Kids 0-7445-6067-5 (p/b) £4.99